DREAM BIG!

Dream small!
Dream any way at all!
Just never forget to dream...

All the unicorns,

Z.W. Mohr

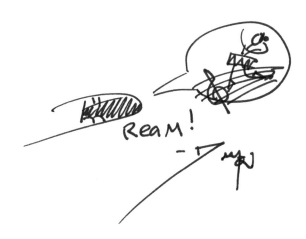

ReaM!
—

Desdemona's Dreams

VOLUME 1

To Dream of Dancing

Written by Z. W. Mohr

Illustrated by Aaron Damon Porter

Desdemona's Dreams LLC - New Orleans

MOHR, Z.W. AND PORTER, AARON DAMON
DESDEMONA'S DREAMS VOLUME I: TO DREAM OF DANCING
WRITTEN BY Z.W. MOHR
AND ILLUSTRATED BY AARON DAMON PORTER
ISBN 978-0-9968874-0-3

DESIGN AND LAYOUT: DARE PORTER, REAL TIME DESIGN
ART PHOTOGRAPHY: MADELEINE WIEAND
Z.W. MOHR PHOTO BY SHADOW ANGELINA
AARON DAMON PORTER PHOTO BY KAULT PHOTOGRAPHY

10 9 8 7 6 5 4 3 2 1

DESDEMONA'S DREAMS LLC
4229 N DERBIGNY STREET
NEW ORLEANS, LOUISIANA 70117

E-MAIL: INFO@DESDEMONASDREAMS.COM

FOR THE DREAMERS . . .
THE WORLD IS WHAT YOU MAKE IT.
~ Z.W. MOHR ~

Prologue

In the town of Remsy there sits a house where the lavender always blooms. A place where the trees are friends in the sunlight, and nightmares in the darkness. None of the townsfolk could say if the house is old, this deep purple Victorian home behind a wrought-iron rose fence. Dog walkers and families walking by gaze at the intricately sculpted iron roses, exquisitely cast down to every thorny detail, but no one would dare touch them. Parents whisper to their children every time they pass, about a little boy who had touched an iron thorn and fallen into a deep sleep that he'd never awakened from. Of course, no one actually knew the child in question, or when that particular whisper began.

Behind the fence a pathway with smooth amethyst stepping stones, beset by an explosion of multicolored sunflowers on either side, winds its way up to the front stoop. The pathway splits like wandering vines around the house to head back towards what everyone

imagines is some sort of storybook kingdom: A backyard where gnomes ride rabbits to gather mushrooms for stew, and sprites fly between giant singing flowers. Since no one has ever actually seen the backyard, the stories have grown even more varied than the colors of sunflowers sown throughout the front.

A gargoyle, carved from dark grey stone, perches above the attic window with a devious toothy grin and a hand outstretched, beckoning people closer with one curved, clawed finger. Thomas Hinkley, the local librarian, swears up and down that he once spotted the statue flying off into the night sky. His claims were met with the gentle "Pshaws," and "You don't says," that the townsfolk use to placate overactive imaginations. Even the town gossip, Ms. Esmerelda Jenkins, exclaimed, "Hinkley's head went looking for his nose in them books, and neither one ever made it out."

But this is neither the story of Thomas Hinkley, nor Esmerelda Jenkins. It is the story of an eleven-year-

old girl named Desdemona living with her aunts, Lulu Ann and Lulu Bell, within the strange purple house in the small town of Remsy. Desdemona, covered in a patchwork quilt, is sound asleep and dreaming. Her teddy bear, appropriately dubbed Teddy, sits next to her head with his eyes ever open and watchful. It's in a dream where this story begins, a dream of fierce sands and fiercer winds, a dream of madness and a song without end . . . .

To Dream of Dancing

A ballerina sways and turns,

Like the whirlwinds

In the sands that burn.

In a castle, in a land,

Where dreams may wander

Just like the sand;

Floating gently through the sky

Lodging fiercely

In someone's eye,

But always moving, never still,

The sands howling as loudly

As a whooping whippoorwill.

Now back to whence this dream began,

To the ballerina

Who moves like whirling sand,

In a ballroom made of stone

With a madman maestro

Composing eldritch songs of the darkest tone.

The dancer is his captive, a dream that strayed too far,

Caught by his web of music

Which trapped her like pits of black tar.

Now, she dances day by night and night by day,

As long as the madman

Continues to play.

The song he plays is devoid of joy,

Filled with the sadness

Of a child's lost toy.

On and on the tune does go,

Never ending, never too fast,

And never, ever too slow.

Then one dream there comes a knock

At the door of this grim stone home

Made of drab grey rock.

The Maestro looks a bit befuddled.

Has another dancer been caught?

Another creature enticed and muddled?

Opening the door to find a girl with eyes so emerald and gay,

And hair that flows like chocolate puddles

On a chocolate raindrop day.

"So, little dream, you've come to dance alongside the other?"

Desdemona looks him in his wild eyes and says,

"Why no sir, I'm her mother."

"She is my dream of dancing and you've stolen her away.

I noticed when I no longer wished

To dance every single day."

With a crazy little chuckle, and a smile quite grim,

The Maestro grabs her by the face

To turn her ear towards him.

"It doesn't matter to me if you think I've done something wrong!

I need the dancer to inspire me,

To help me finish my song."

With this he closes the door in Desdemona's face.

She can hear the Maestro yelling,

Warning the ballerina to keep up the pace.

Desdemona walks back and forth, angry at the Maestro's disdain.

She can't just leave her dream of dancing

In the care of one so cruel and insane.

Back and forth she paces outside the door,

Her nostrils flaring,

Eyes darting to and fro like those of a wild boar.

Trying to think of a clever plan,

Knowing every moment that passes

Means her dream is a slave of that awful man.

Turning and spinning for that crazed buffoon,

With his wild, yellow, bloodshot eyes,

And hair puffed out like a loon.

Exasperated, Desdemona screams at the sky,

"I don't know what to do!

I fear my dream of dancing is going to die."

Then back to the waking world she goes

Where eyes must stay open

And dreams must lay low.

Teddy and The Aunts

In the purple house, in the small town of Remsy, Desdemona bolts awake with tears streaming down her face, humming a strange garbled tune.

"Teddy! Oh Teddy!" She cries out, embracing her friend and confidant bear. "What should I do?"

Teddy hugs her back and comfortingly pats Desdemona's shoulder. "Calm now, my Lady. You are safely at home where no one will harm you. Tell me of your dream so I may counsel you in the right course of action."

Desdemona props herself up and wipes the tears from her eyes, her chocolate-brown hair pooling upon the deep purple pillows as she relates the ballerina's dilemma.

"He was some sort of crazy maestro, and he was holding my dream of dancing captive so that he could finish a song. She was dying, Teddy. I could feel her getting weaker and weaker as she danced for him. I know I

was dreaming, but it was so real. As the ballerina grew weaker, something inside of me felt like it was breaking."

Teddy jumps down from the bed and starts pacing furiously, his furry paw rubbing his chin as he paces back and forth.

"Aha! I have it," Teddy utters in his deep bear voice, which used to surprise Desdemona since he is so cuddly looking. At that same moment comes a knock at the door. A voice as singsong as a bluebird comes warbling in as Desdemona's Aunt Lulu Ann flits through the entrance. She is tall, with hair the color of spun gold that always shimmers, as if sunlight is peeking through some unseen window. A ruby-lipped smile never falters from her lips, and even her reprimands bring welcome giggles. A number of men and women about town have been known to say,

"You haven't yet seen the sunrise until you've seen Miss Lulu Ann."

"Time to rise and shine, my dove! There's toast with blueberry ginger jam and apple sausages waiting to be eaten. Your red boots and rainbow dress are laid out upon the chair for you." As she says this, Aunt Lulu Ann waves her hand in the direction of the big red-cushioned reading chair in the corner of Desdemona's room.

Desdemona doesn't remember her clothes being there before, but both of her aunts do that kind of thing all the time, so it doesn't really surprise her when objects appear where her aunts say they should be.

"I'll get dressed and come right down. Has Aunt Lulu Bell come downstairs yet?" Desdemona asks, hoping the answer is "No."

"No, my sweet. She's still in that dusty attic she calls a room, probably imagining new ways to pull the wings off flies and then who she should feed them to." Aunt Lulu Ann chuckles at her last statement and then leaves the room.

"You don't really think that's what Aunt Lulu Bell is doing, do you Teddy?" Desdemona asks as she gets up and changes from her purple nightgown into her rainbow dress.

"I wouldn't put it past her," Teddy mutters.

"Huh?"

"I'm sure she's still sleeping," he says loud enough for her to hear this time.

Desdemona finishes dressing and then checks her rather enormous doll house to make

sure her dolls haven't wandered off in the middle of the night again. They'd wandered off once before and she'd found them outside having tea in the garden. Seeing that they are still tucked into their beds sleeping, Desdemona grabs her bright red leather book bag with a picture of a ballerina on its flap, hugs Teddy, and heads downstairs. She passes Aunt Lulu Bell's door on the way to the staircase, trying not to look at its creepy carvings of faces frozen in terror. When she reaches the staircase, Desdemona looks around to make sure neither of her

aunts is watching, then she slides down the banister giggling.

After reaching the bottom of the staircase, Desdemona turns left into the library, one of her favorite rooms in the house. The library has three large comfortable chairs very similar to the one in her bedroom. Each chair has a reading lamp behind it made of brass, and two walls lined with nine shelves of books each. Her stomach issues a warning growl for her not to dawdle, so she carries on through the archway leading into the dining room, where steaming apple sausages and blueberry-gingered toast sit waiting on a plate. After devouring her breakfast, she waves to the moving frescos on the walls. A knight in full armor having tea with a red dragon both wave back at her as she grabs her book bag from the back of the chair and heads towards the front door. Aunt Lulu Ann stands waiting by the door to see Desdemona off with a packed lunch that she tucks into Desdemona's book bag.

School Daze

"Now, remember to pay attention in class. Daydream only when the teacher isn't talking, and try not to talk to the other kids about our home."

"I won't," Desdemona says, frowning at the memory of how much the other kids had laughed at her when she'd insisted that her teddy bear really did talk.

Opening the front door, she skips down the walkway, waves once more at her aunt before heading out the iron-rose gate, and makes her way down the sidewalk of their maple-tree-lined street. She says "Hello" to each tree she passes; their gnarled branches always make her think of outstretched arms waiting to help her climb. As she reaches the last tree, Desdemona lets out a sigh, knowing she's skipped the three blocks to her school, which sits in front of her with its dingy yellow walls, brown bricks, and black shingle roof.

There isn't anything inviting about Greyson Drab Elementary School. Everything in the schoolyard is

either concrete or dirt, the playground being nothing more than a solid blacktop backdrop with a chain link fence surrounding the whole thing. Desdemona loves learning and playing, but it feels like those things happen more often in her dreams or with Teddy, and classes have become harder because her attention wanders more and more with every passing year. Her teachers seem to have lost their love of teaching, spouting off facts with so little interest that it is tiring just to hear them, and the children have begun to lose their desire to play games or do anything requiring imagination. It probably doesn't help that she has a hard time making friends. The other kids often look at her as if she's some creature from another planet, and it gets worse and worse with each new grade. Some of them have taken to calling her "Daydreamer" or "Silly Heart," because she often plays games by herself with just her imagination to keep her company. One time she asked this other girl, Ermda Reven, what she dreamt about. Desdemona thought that, because Ermda usually sat alone, maybe they could be friends.

Ermda, with her frizzy red hair, freckled face, thick glasses, and grey clothing that still didn't seem to match even though it was usually all shades of one color. There was always the dour look of one who takes everything too seriously on Ermda's face, and she'd responded to Desdemona's question by glaring at her and saying, "What's the point of dreaming?"

When she'd asked her aunts if it was bad to dream, make up stories, and play games, they'd just ignored her questions and started asking her about the other children's behavior. Aunt Lulu Bell dismissed her further questioning with a claw-like finger saying, "Of course you should be using your imagination. You're certainly going to need it in the future."

Aunt Lulu Ann had smiled sharply at her sister when she'd said this, but then told Desdemona, "Just go play in the garden with Teddy, beautiful girl. There are adventures eagerly awaiting your attention, and you wouldn't want to disappoint them."

A bell wakes Desdemona from her memories and she runs up the stairs, now late for her first class. It is her least favorite class, Etiquette 1A, taught by her least favorite teacher, Ms. Kaputski. As she races into the classroom, Ms. Kaputski steps in front of her – her teacher's salt-and-pepper hair pulled back tightly into a bun, with horn-rimmed glasses too big for her head over catlike green eyes. She always wears a grey tweed jacket with a matching skirt, a white blouse, and what she refers

to as 'sensible shoes'. In fact, the only thing colorful about Ms. Kaputski is her eyes, which are currently staring disapprovingly at Desdemona.

"I'm glad you could join us, young lady," says Ms. Kaputski with a sneer on her face. "You know how rude it is to be late?"

"Very rude, for girls trying to grow up to be proper ladies," replies Desdemona, looking down and trying to seem contrite.

"Well, at least you've learned something. At recess I want you to go to the music room and write, 'I will not be late', one hundred times on the chalkboard. Mr. Harrison's chalkboard in the music room is bigger than ours and should be able to provide you with ample space for this task."

Before Desdemona can even complain about her punishment, Ms. Kaputski screeches, "TO YOUR SEAT!"

Desdemona marches to the back of the class, puts her books, pens, and pencils inside her desk, and lays her book bag across the back of her chair, trying hard to ignore the snickers of her classmates.

As Ms. Kaputski begins the lesson about how you are supposed to properly address married and unmarried people in a civilized world, Desdemona's mind starts to wander. She can hear all of the other children trying to take notes in their notebooks - the scratching of pencils against paper, the teacher droning on while facing the chalkboard writing the proper "honorific" titles to address adults by, and the "Tick . . . Tock" of the clock in the room. It makes her think of the metronome on the piano in their sitting room at home.

"Tick . . . Tock . . . Tick . . . Tock . . ."

Pencils scratching back and forth, Desdemona's eyes are beginning to close bit by bit. An image of the ballerina in a deep red leotard and skirt dancing feverishly appears in her mind.

"Tick . . . Tock . . . Tick . . . Tock . . ."

A Dangerous Agreement

Then, through the haze she can hear it again.

That maddening dark tune,

The one without end.

Suddenly feeling the chill of wind in her bones

And smelling the dust

As it clings to the stone.

Wafting through the air like a whiff of freshly baked pie,

She can hear the crazy melody

And the mad Maestro's cries.

"Dance pretty dancer, dance without care!

I feel that the ending

Is almost there."

Then the ballerina stops with a tear in her eye,

"Oh please, sir, I'm tired.

If I dance much more I'll die."

With a slam of the keys and the Maestro's hard stare

She feels as if frost

Has suddenly filled the air.

"If your death is what it takes, then your death is just fine.

All that matters is ending my masterpiece

And that the ending be divine."

"NOOOOO!" Desdemona screams at the loon.

"I'll help you finish your song,

Your mad crazy tune."

The Maestro looks grimly at the girl, then back at the dancer.

Desdemona nervously taps her left foot

As she waits for his answer.

"Alright, you persistent wretch of a girl,

But, if you fail then you're both mine to command

As dancers in my world."

Desdemona sees the ballerina's violet eyes glimmering with tears.

Thinking of all the wondrous dances she'd been taught in her dreams

Her anger overwhelms any rising fears.

Desdemona glares at him with fire in her eyes.

"I agree to your terms. How long do I have

To bring about your wicked song's final demise?"

The Maestro cackles as he snaps his hand out with a flare,

Pulling an ornate hourglass

Out of thin air.

"For a lady so clever, as I'm sure you must be,

Twenty minutes should be plenty of time,

But, I'll be generous and give you that times three."

Desdemona begins to say, "I'm clever, I agree…."

"Ha! I heard you agree." He spins about

Laughing with glee.

"When these sands all reach bottom, your time shall be done."

Turning it over, he tosses it to Desdemona

And says, "Now won't this be fun!"

"Wait, how much time is in here?" Desdemona asks in a surprised voice.

The Maestro just sneers and says,

"It doesn't really matter, you've already agreed to this choice."

The ballerina gasps as she starts to complain,

When right at that moment

Desdemona snaps awake again.

A Crash of Inspiration

"DESDEMONA!" yells Ms. Kaputski.

"Daydreaming in my class again. First, you're rude enough to be late, and then you don't even pay attention." Her teacher is fuming.

"I'm sorry, Ms. Kaputski," Desdemona says, trying to slide further down into her chair. Something she hadn't

noticed in her right hand slips out of her fingers and falls to the floor with a CLINK!

"And what was that?!" Ms. Kaputski shouts.

In-between her feet she can see a small ornate hourglass.

"How is that possible?" Desdemona wonders. She'd never brought something out of her dreams before.

"Well? Are you going to tell me what fell, or do I have to come over there?" Ms. Kaputski growls.

"Just my pen," Desdemona replies as she reaches down and grabs the hourglass from between her feet.

"Untimely, a poor listener, and now clumsy too. What kind of a lady could you ever hope to be? Add fifty more lines to your punishment, daydreamer." Ms. Kaputski says the word 'daydreamer' with such venom that Desdemona flinches.

"I'll do better, I promise." Desdemona cowers.

"See that you do!" Ms. Kaputski shouts as she turns back to the chalkboard and starts writing again.

Desdemona looks up at the time, realizing she still has about forty minutes of class left before their morning snack break. What had the Maestro said? He'd said she would have twenty minutes times three? An hour. She would get an hour to figure out the ending to his song. Taking another look at the hour glass in her hands she tries to turn it every which way, realizing that the sands only flow in one direction.

When class finally comes to an end Desdemona leaps from her seat, grabs her book bag with the hour glass now tucked inside of it, and runs out the door.

"Don't forget your…" Ms. Kaputski starts to yell, but Desdemona cuts her off with a shout as she bolts from class: "I'm going to the music room!"

She runs down the hall until she sees room 248; the music teacher is locking the door. Mr. Harrison is an older man with caramel skin and silvery long hair. He always dresses in bright sweaters and crisp black pants and teaches every class with the exuberance that comes

from loving what he does. In fact, Mr. Harrison is the only teacher she has who still encourages the kids to have fun in the classroom. When Desdemona runs up to the door, Mr. Harrison doesn't even notice her, being too immersed in the tune he is whistling to himself.

"Wait! Ms. Kaputski wants me to write on your chalkboard over break that I won't be late again to class," she blurts out while trying to catch her breath.

"Well, we best not both get on Ms. Kaputski's bad side then, eh?" Mr. Harrison replies in his slight Jamaican lilt, and with a wink he opens the door for her. Mr. Harrison is always really kind to Desdemona. He often tells her about the Mocho Mountains of Jamaica where he is from and ends almost every story with, "Only dreamers make music that really means anything." Then he chuckles to himself and starts to hum some old tune she doesn't recognize.

"Lock the door behind you when you're done. And remember that you only have twenty minutes."

Realizing how right Mr. Harrison truly is, Desdemona decides to start with the piano. Trying to remember the lessons Aunt Lulu Ann has given her, she sets the hourglass on top of the piano and sits down at the keys to try and finish the Maestro's song.

She remembers the tune pretty well, but is having a hard time recreating it. Missing a note here and there, not able to think of the direction it should go in – why did she think she could do this? Now her dream of dancing will not only die, but she might die alongside the dancer in that crazy Maestro's world. Slamming the keys one last time, Desdemona stands up from the piano, exasperated. Looking at the wall clock and then the hourglass, she realizes there are only five minutes left in the break.

Desdemona glances over at the woodwinds, and the string instruments right next to them. Maybe one of those can help finish this song. As she runs towards them she fails to notice a pair of cymbals on the floor and ends up slipping and sliding on top of a cymbal and into a drum set with a loud crash. Sitting on the floor, a little dazed, it suddenly becomes clear to Desdemona how to end the Maestro's song. Hopefully she will be able to take something into her dream as easily as she brought something out.

Laying down on the floor of the music room with the hourglass in one hand and the pair of cymbals under her arm, Desdemona lets herself drift off. Thinking of the sound of the metronome again, hearing the gentle tick tock of the music room's clock, sleep finally begins to take hold with only a few minutes to spare.

The Last Dance

Desdemona materializes before the Maestro, a stony look on his face.

"I see you have enough sand left

For me to play my song just once in our little race."

Desdemona readies her cymbals and says, "So play then, you loon.

I've discovered a way

To end your shoddy tune!"

With an angry "HARUMPH!" he starts playing the piano keys

Glaring at Desdemona and the dancer,

Who now has trembling knees.

Such a fury is loosed that the windows shake,

And at the height of the song a loud crash reverberates

Making the very air around them feel as if it's going to break.

The Maestro plays on, caught up in his crazy song,

Hearing crashes and bangs

As his fingers run along.

Desdemona dances around the piano,

Constantly changing the intensity

With which she clangs the cymbals to and fro,

Smiling when she feels the end is near,

Having beaten him at his own game

And conquered any fear.

When he comes to the part that hadn't been finished

A final crash resounds

And his mad hands fall away, diminished.

"What have you done?" The Maestro's lips quivered.

"I finished your song.

My end of our deal has certainly been delivered."

Desdemona reaches over and grasps one of the dancer's hands.

"Follow me, ballerina.

Let me take you away from this crazy old man."

The Maestro sits there with tears running down his cheeks.

He mumbles out something,

But no one can hear it, for it comes out too weak.

Desdemona and her dream dancer, walking hand in hand,

Disappear from the dingy stone castle

Leaving the Maestro alone in his desolate land of sand.

Behind the Curtain

While Desdemona frees her dream of dancing, Aunt Lulu Ann and Aunt Lulu Bell sit in the library of their home in Remsy poring over ancient tomes, each text filled with writing that shifts and moves, sometimes forming pictures before transforming back into words of some language older than the moon.

"How has our niece done?" croaks Aunt Lulu Bell, dust falling off her black robes as a boney, crooked finger turns another page.

"Even better than expected, with a certain flare and panache that I believe she gets from me," Aunt Lulu Ann replies with a whimsical smile.

"Our brother often had a flare for the dramatic as well. Don't forget, that's what got us into this mess in the first place," chides Aunt Lulu Bell.

"Yes, well, Desdemona should be ready to face some greater challenges now. I believe it's your turn to set her in the right direction. Maybe give her a day or two of celebration, before showing her the way to Mar. Let her go into that mess with a lightness to her step."

Aunt Lulu Bell shuts the tome on her lap and glares at her sister, "You always like to paint the picture to be prettier than it is, don't you. The road ahead is long and dark and she'll not love you any more for deceptions, no matter how pleasant they may seem. You'll see, my sister, that the blunt truth of a nightmare will far outweigh the false niceties of a well-crafted daydream."

To be continued . . .

Z.W. Mohr was born in the foothills of Los Angeles, between a wild blaze and a mudslide. Being raised on stories told by firelight, and traveling to hidden temples of long gone civilizations at a young age, might have unlocked doors of imagination he's never learned how to close. Knowing that the best castles are built from dreams, he learned the masonry of language so he could build castles of his own. The stories of Desdemona are an invitation to visit these castles. Please pack lightly. Wear your heart on your sleeve so that the gatekeeper knows it's you, keep a secret in your pocket to trade for treasure, and leave this realm only when you have your own dream to go to.

Acknowledgements

There are so many people whose love and support have gone into the creation of this tale. Without their help, my dream might have foundered. Thanks to: my mother – you taught me the love of story and art, and I'm sure you're still telling tales wherever you are now; my father for gifting me with a strong and loving heart, and telling me to find my happiness; my brother Jim for encouraging me to live the life I choose; my niece Selina and nephew Sean – this story has more to do with you than you will ever know, and like you both, it too shall grow; my Casey for picking me up, brushing me off, and telling me to never stop writing – you are my moon; Dave Lundquist and Wendy Coren for their healing hands, encouraging words, and friendship; Carin Chapman for her keen eye, advice, and providing a face for Desdemona; Nick Fox for a suggestion that changed the course of this story's creation; Aaron Porter for his artistic vision, friendship, and desire to put stories into the world with me; Dare Porter for his amazing design skills and willingness to help in the birthing; all of the friends that have encouraged my imagination; and last, but never least, to all of the dreamers who gave their stories to the world before me so that new dreams could be inspired by theirs.

Aaron Damon Porter, born in Oakland, California, learned quickly that Mr. Sketch scented markers are not, in fact, edible. Inspired by Bill Watterson's Calvin and Hobbes, N.C. Wyeth's work in *Treasure Island*, and David Mack's re-imagining of Daredevil, Mr. Porter has worked on his own translations of the inner and outer worlds we inhabit. Painting full-time in New Orleans since 2008, he has developed bright but silent worlds of his own. *Desdemona's Dreams* is his first foray into fairytale illustration. The creative endeavors of Mr. Mohr and Mr. Porter in this dreamscape with Desdemona and Teddy is proving A Most Exciting Adventure.

Acknowledgements

"Genius is in the synthesis of information." – *gob-smacking wisdom from a friend.*

I'm proud of my work, and I couldn't have done it alone. Whether through fervent conversations, or a Herculean hand-of-assistance, every brush stroke herein owes thanks to those who believe in me. If we ever shared a moon, spinning fine filaments of creative conjecture, consider yourself thanked.

And then, there are those super-human pillars of love and support: Thank you to my father, Dare, who kept me flush in paper and pens, introduced me to Picasso at the age of five, and has been an all-around stellar dad. (He is our layout guru and I thank him sincerely on the professional level as well.) Thank you also to my mother, Molly, for her love, support, and education – and for her hawk-like editing eye; to my dear friends, Zach and Casey, whose hospitality is a thing of wonder, and whose unconditional love I return with deep joy; to my dear friend and love, Phlaurel, for still being interested and enthusiastic about every nuance of my work; to Otter and Alma, my long-john friend and her daughter, who have distilled in me the whatfors of tale-telling; and sincere hugs and thanks to the grounding presence of Sophia, Kara, and all the beasts.

CPSIA information can be obtained
at www.ICGtesting.com
Printed in the USA
LVIC06n0842290916
506636LV00002B/3